Strega Nona
and
the Twins

Written and illustrated by
Tomie dePaola

Ready-to-Read

Simon Spotlight
New York   London   Toronto   Sydney   New Delhi

"Hello, Strega Nona!
Hello, Bambolona and
Big Anthony!"
said Signora Clara.

"Thank you for looking after the twins today while I go to the market."

"The twins caused so much trouble at the market last week that they are not allowed there anymore," whispered Strega Nona.

"Big Anthony, take them into the field to help you. Bambolona and I are going to clean the house."

"I will go,"
said Bambolona.

"Children, time to come
into the house,"
called Strega Nona.

"Thank goodness for that, Bambolona," said Big Anthony.

"I hope Strega Nona knows
what she is in for,"
said Bambolona.
"I am going to go watch."
"Me too,"
said Big Anthony.

"Look, Bambolona,"
Big Anthony whispered.
"Strega Nona made a
magic potion!"

"Look, Big Anthony," Bambolona whispered. "Strega Nona is saying a magic spell!"

"Thank you, Strega Nona.
Thank you, Bambolona
and Big Anthony,"
said Signora Clara.

"It was no trouble,"
said Strega Nona.

"We saw you give the twins a magic potion, Strega Nona," said Bambolona.

"And we heard you say
a spell from your magic
book!" said Big Anthony.

"Don't be silly,
my children,"
said Strega Nona.

"I gave them warm milk
with honey and read them
a bedtime story from my
book of tales. That is
magic enough."

For Tom, Lucinda, Eli, and Leslie.
They'll know why!

SIMON SPOTLIGHT
An imprint of Simon & Schuster Children's Publishing Division
1230 Avenue of the Americas, New York, New York 10020
This Simon Spotlight edition May 2017
Text and illustrations copyright © 2017 by Tomie dePaola
All rights reserved, including the right of reproduction in whole or in part in any form.
SIMON SPOTLIGHT, READY-TO-READ, and colophon are registered trademarks of Simon & Schuster, Inc.
For information about special discounts for bulk purchases, please contact Simon & Schuster Special Sales at
1-866-506-1949 or business@simonandschuster.com.
Manufactured in the United States of America 0317 LAK
2 4 6 8 10 9 7 5 3 1
Library of Congress Control Number 2017932250
ISBN 978-1-4814-8138-0 (hc)
ISBN 978-1-4814-8137-3 (pbk)
ISBN 978-1-4814-8139-7 (eBook)